The
Queen's Maid

MORE RACING READS:

Invasion
by June Crebbin

Daisy Dawson and the Big Freeze
by Steve Voake

Flotsam and Jetsam and the Stormy Surprise
by Tanya Landman

Big Dog Bonnie
by Bel Mooney

Anna Hibiscus
by Atinuke

Hooray for Anna Hibiscus!
by Atinuke

The No. 1 Car Spotter
by Atinuke

Emily's Surprising Voyage
by Sue Purkiss

Miracle on Separation Street
by Bob Graham

Oshie
by Jon Blake

JUNE CREBBIN

The Queen's Maid

illustrated by James de la Rue

**WALKER
BOOKS**

First published 2012 by Walker Books Ltd
87 Vauxhall Walk, London SE11 5HJ

2 4 6 8 10 9 7 5 3 1

Text © 2012 June Crebbin
Illustrations © 2012 James de la Rue

This book has been typeset in StempelSchneidler

Printed and bound in Great Britain by Clays Ltd, St Ives plc

British Library Cataloguing in Publication Data:
a catalogue record for this book is available from the British Library

ISBN 978-1-4063-2581-2

www.walker.co.uk

For Carol in Kalamazoo

J.C.

For Amy

J.D.

The Royal Visit

Jane spurred her mare on, up the hill. Delphine responded readily, surging forward in an extra burst of speed and Jane laughed out loud in excitement.

No matter that she, Lady Jane Hargrave of Carrington Manor in the county of Dorsetshire, should not be out on her new pony. No matter that it wasn't seemly to be riding astride like any peasant woman. Soon she would reach the crest of the hill and be able to see for herself the approaching royal procession.

For weeks, the whole household had been getting ready for this moment. Every room in the house had been swept, scrubbed and dusted. Carpenters and painters had been employed to repair and restore all items of furniture. Vast supplies of rushes had been ordered to ensure fresh daily covering for the floors.

But now the manor stood ready to receive a queen: the Queen of England, Her gracious Majesty, Elizabeth!

At the top of the hill, Jane drew Delphine to a halt. The mare, reluctant to stop, skittered about but Jane steadied her long enough to see the procession winding its way ever closer towards the manor. Down below, glittering in the sunlight, was the newly dug-out lake where, that night, for the very first time, a pageant was to take place. There would be actors and musicians, songs and speeches. Jane could hardly wait.

The preparations for the Queen's royal progress, as it was called, had cost Jane's parents a fortune. What was more, the family had been obliged to move into the gatehouse, since all the rooms in Carrington Manor were required for the Queen's courtiers, advisors and servants.

"It's expected," Jane's father had told her when she complained. It was also necessary for the Queen to receive expensive presents, and certainly Tempest – the magnificent white stallion that was even now munching his hay in the manor stables – had cost a pretty penny.

Jane already adored him. Every day since he had arrived, she had slipped in to offer him treats, a carrot or two or an apple. He always whinnied at her approach.

Jane wrenched her thoughts away from the stallion and gave herself to the matter in hand. She knew she had to be at her

mother's side when the Queen arrived.
Suddenly, Jane regretted coming out.
She didn't want to cause her mother distress
by being late. Lady Anne had worked so
hard to prepare the house for the royal visit.

She turned Delphine and rode swiftly
downhill, skirting round the moat to enter
by the rear gate. That way, she knew,
would be quicker. But even as she thrust
Delphine's reins into a waiting groom's
hands, she heard the clatter of a hundred
horses arriving in the main
courtyard at the front
of the house.

Picking up her skirts,
she ran, pausing once
to snatch up some
fresh blooms as
she passed through
the flower
gardens.

There was no time to change. As Jane rushed through the house to take her place in the courtyard, she wished she hadn't stayed out so long. Her mother looked pale and anxious.

A carriage drew up. A footman opened the door. Out stepped the Queen.

Jane gasped. She had never seen Her Majesty in real life, only in portraits. She was not prepared for the ghost-like whiteness of the Queen's face or the startling red hair piled high on her head.

Jane's father, who had ridden out to the county boundary to meet the Queen, dismounted.

"Welcome to my home, Your Majesty," he said, bowing. "Allow me to introduce my wife."

Lady Anne performed a deep curtsy and murmured a few words.

Now or never, thought Jane. She stepped forward. From behind her skirts she produced a bunch of sweet-smelling gilly-flowers and offered them to the Queen.

"May your visit here be as glorious as these blooms and as bright as the sun that opened them," she said in Latin.

Looking up through her eyelashes, Jane could tell that the Queen was impressed. She nodded graciously, accepted the posy, thanked Jane and proceeded into the manor.

Later, back in the gatehouse, Jane sat and waited. She couldn't settle. She dreaded harsh words from her father, or worse, gentle reproaches from her mother. Suppose her parents were so angry at her late, untidy appearance that they forbade her to attend the pageant?

But as the afternoon wore on, nothing was said; nothing happened except that a maidservant was sent to help Jane get dressed and to arrange her hair. Jane was so relieved that she sat still through all the smoothing and tucking, the curling and pinning. What a fuss! But as she entered the great hall that evening, she realized why.

She was to sit next to the Queen!

"Mind your manners," whispered her mother, "and speak not with your mouth full."

Jane sat on the Queen's left. Opposite were various ladies of the court, all looking

down their noses at Jane. On her other side sat a stern-looking gentleman who spoke to the Queen over Jane's head as though she wasn't there.

But the Queen addressed Jane often, sometimes in Latin, sometimes in French, sometimes Italian. She expressed her delight in Jane's ability to understand, and reply, in all three.

"I like learning languages," Jane told her, trying not to speak with her mouth full of delicious spit-roasted chicken.

The Queen wanted to know more about Jane's activities.

"I enjoy playing the lute and the virginals," Jane replied. "But above all I love to ride my pony and to act."

The Queen's sharp black eyes glinted. "Acting?" she said. "Surely not."

Jane knew that women and girls were not allowed to act. "Only with my brothers and sisters," she said quickly. A thought struck her. "Would Your Majesty care to see one of my plays?"

"Ah," said the Queen. "I fear there may not be time enough. But certainly we could ride together."

"Wait till you see…" Jane began. She had almost blurted out the secret that was waiting in the stables!

The Queen raised her eyebrows. "What shall I see?"

But Jane was saved from answering by the arrival of strawberries and cream. What a relief! The Earl would not have been happy if Jane had given away his surprise.

After the meal, everyone processed down to the lake to watch the pageant. Attired as Tritons, members of the household were swimming in the water, blowing a fanfare on their trumpets. Behind them came a boat drawn by Neptune, the god of the sea, accompanied by six maidens dressed as nymphs and singing. Jane, seated next to the Queen, could barely keep still for excitement. She knew all the songs – she had written two of them! She sang along under her breath.

Next came more boats bedecked with flowers and all manner of musicians. Jane's mother laid a restraining hand on her daughter to keep her from leaping to her feet and shouting joyous approval. But the Queen only smiled.

As darkness fell, rockets exploded into the sky, fireballs scudded across the water, and on every bank coloured firewheels whirled round and round.

A night to remember, thought Jane sleepily as she tumbled into bed. And tomorrow…

The following morning, a crowd gathered in the main courtyard to witness the presentation of the Earl's gift. Jane couldn't wait to see the Queen's face.

Wearing a green velvet dress, Queen Elizabeth appeared at the door. Tempest was brought forward. The crowd hushed. The great horse

tossed his head and pawed the ground.

The Earl addressed the Queen, saying that he hoped she would accept this small token of his esteem.

The Queen expressed her thanks. "He is a noble steed," she said.

"Perhaps this afternoon Your Majesty would like to try him at the hunt?" suggested the Earl.

"I should like to try him now," declared the Queen.

"But the travelling players are here," said the Earl, more than a little flustered. "They have a new play especially written for Your Majesty."

"Time enough," said the Queen sharply. She could not take her eyes off the great horse. "Saddle him up," she commanded and waved a hand towards Jane. "Your daughter may accompany me."

19

Jane almost flew to the stables. What a privilege to be chosen to ride with the Queen of England!

When she brought Delphine out to the yard, the Queen was already seated. Tempest shook his head, snatching at the reins, stamping and snorting.

"He is perhaps a little fiery," said Jane's father nervously. "If only you would allow someone to go with you…"

The Queen laughed. "Do not concern yourself, my lord. I like a horse with spirit!" She wheeled her mount around and sped out through the archway, leaving the whole household staring.

Jane urged Delphine forwards, clattering past the maids of honour, who stood open-mouthed but silenced.

On the grassy slopes beside the lake,
the Queen urged Tempest into a gallop.
Delphine was only too keen to pursue. It
was like flying, thought Jane. She was rarely
encouraged to ride as fast, even following
the hunt. At the furthest point of the lake,
the Queen slowed Tempest to a walk.

"Where now?" she asked.

"Uphill!" cried Jane.

It was a glorious ride. Jane saw that the
Queen was indeed a fine horsewoman,
just as she had heard. Though Tempest
shied more than once when birds flew up
suddenly out of the hedgerow, or dogs
barked at them, the Queen
remained in control.

Eventually, the Queen declared they must return. Jane couldn't help feeling sad, but as they came in sight of the manor, a trumpet sounded. The travelling players, of course! Their cart was set up as a stage in the courtyard and already the audience had taken its place at the windows of the house.

The Queen elected to watch from the balcony of her chamber and Jane was told to accompany her.

There was just time to assure the Earl that all had gone well on the ride before the play began.

The main story was about a beautiful and brave queen, and jesters and acrobats added colour and fun to the spectacle. As she was watching, Jane suddenly had an idea for her own play. She determined to write it down the minute the midday meal was over.

But it was not to be. As soon as Jane had finished eating, she was summoned to the royal chambers to play the lute while the Queen rested. She was furious. She flung herself into the playing with passion, but at the Queen's steely gaze, she tempered the tune to a quieter mood.

Every day that followed, Jane was summoned into the Queen's presence. Sometimes it was to ride; sometimes it was to walk with Her Majesty around the gardens, conversing on subjects of the Queen's choosing; sometimes it was to read plays aloud to her.

On the last day of the visit, Lady Sara, one of the maids of honour, came to the gatehouse before breakfast requesting Jane's attendance.

"But I was just going to ride!" objected

Jane. She appealed to her mother.

"Please inform the Queen that Lady Jane will attend her at once," said Lady Anne, giving Jane a stern look. Lady Sara curtsied and left, making no effort to conceal the look of amusement on her face.

"They're a bunch of ninnies, those maids of honour," said Jane, thrusting her arms into the close-fitting sleeves of her dress. "They're always simpering and giggling and talking behind my back."

"Maybe they're a little jealous," said her mother gently. "The Queen has taken such a liking to you and they haven't been needed." She hugged her daughter and bade her make haste.

Jane hurried to the manor. Of course, it was wonderful to have the Queen of England staying in her house. But it was also bothersome. I'm not her servant, thought Jane.

She was ushered into the Queen's private chamber and she curtsied. Her Majesty smiled, and greeted Jane warmly.

"So, Jane, my visit is almost at an end. I have been pleased with your company and your conduct."

Jane made as if to reply, but the Queen held up her hand.

"Therefore," she went on, "I have decided that you shall become my sixth maid of honour."

Jane was silenced. Attend the Queen? Do her every bidding? Leave Carrington Manor?

"Naturally," continued the Queen, a note of impatience creeping into her voice, "you are speechless at the honour bestowed upon you. But what have you to say?"

Jane struggled to find her voice. "No," she blurted out at last. "I cannot."

The Queen's expression changed. "Why so?" she demanded.

"My mother has need of me," said Jane.

The Queen's face relaxed. "Do not concern yourself, child. Your mother has already consented. Lady Anne is overjoyed at your good fortune. Now" – she waved her away – "see to it that all is made ready."

The day passed in a whirl. Jane's mother assured her that to be received at court, especially at such a young age, was an opportunity offered to few. "I'm so proud of you," she said.

"But I'll miss you," wailed Jane. "I'll miss all of you. And what about my studies and my music – and my pony?"

Her entreaties were in vain. Shortly before sunrise the following morning, Queen Elizabeth and her entourage, including Lady Jane Hargrave, set out for London.

Heavens!

Jane lay in bed listening to the soft, even breathing around her. She could not sleep, even though she was exhausted after the long tiring journey from home. Misery swept over her as she remembered afresh that this was home now: Whitehall Palace in the heart of London.

Already she hated it. She had hated the noise and stink of the city as they'd ridden through the narrow streets. She had hated the crowds that had stared and shouted. As for the other maids of honour, only Katherine had shown any sign of friendship. The rest had teased her all the way, describing the various duties she would have to perform. It was all very well her mother saying she was one of the most fortunate girls in the realm: she didn't feel it.

Jane turned onto her side. At least Delphine had been allowed to accompany her. Though Jane had been tormented even over that. "Why should she have a special mount?" Sara had complained the minute they'd set off. "We have to be content with amblers and riding pillion."

Lady Katherine had ventured to remark that she was only too glad to be seated on a nice, steady ambler, behind a groom who controlled it much better than she ever could. But she had been laughed at by the others.

Jane fell at last into an uneasy slumber but

it seemed she was woken almost at once by Mrs Norris, the Mistress in Charge of the maids of honour. "Come, my lady," she said. "The Queen expects you."

Jane struggled into her clothes. Even though it was hardly daylight, the Queen was already being attended to in her bedchamber. Jane entered hesitantly with the others. Nervously, she sat on the edge of her seat, wondering what her first duty would be. To her surprise, she found she was not required to do anything except make polite conversation. The Queen's servants dressed her. They smoothed a white paste over her face and dusted it with a fine powder. Then they arranged her hair and fixed it in place with precious jewels.

It all took a very long time and Jane had to stifle more than one yawn. She was relieved when everything was completed to the Queen's satisfaction and the whole company proceeded to morning prayers.

After breakfast, the Queen retired to her private chambers to consult with her ministers. "The King of Spain is causing trouble again," Mrs Norris explained when the other maids of honour had left. "They say he's preparing a fleet of warships, an armada, and plans to invade us!" She sniffed. "The Queen won't have that." She swept away, leaving Jane wondering what to do next. She supposed she had better return to her rooms but she had no idea in which direction to go.

She opened a door and found herself in a long passage. At the far end, another door opened. Jane felt the rush of fresh air. A servant came through and the door closed.

Jane made her way towards it and in a
moment was outside in the palace grounds.

No one had told her what to do, so surely
it would be all right to find the stables – and
Delphine. Her heart leapt at the thought.

Formal gardens stretched before her. Jane
hurried down a path, aiming for an archway
in the hedge. On the other side, she found
kitchen gardens, and beyond them,
she could see the stable block.

When she finally found Delphine, a groom
was with her.

"How is she?" asked Jane. "It was a very
long journey."

"She's a strong little mare," replied the
boy. "She's well."

Jane watched him check Delphine's hooves,
comb her mane and brush out her tail. She
liked the way he talked to her as he worked,
was gentle but firm when he asked her to
move over and patted her when she obeyed.

Jane asked the boy what his name was.

"Kit," he replied.

"Will you always be in charge of Delphine?" asked Jane.

"Yes, my lady. That is, until I go to my new job."

"Oh," said Jane, disappointed. "When is that to be?"

"I'm not sure," said Kit. "As soon as I get word from my friend Will. He works at the new theatre on Bankside across the river. When people arrive on horseback, he looks after their horses while they watch the play. But he's writing a play so he wants me to take over his job. He wants to work *inside* the theatre!"

"I like to write plays," Jane told him.

"You should meet Will," said Kit. "He's never without a pen in his hand!" He gave Delphine one last pat and stood back. "Please excuse me, my lady. I have to see to the other horses now."

*　　*　　*

In the days that followed, Jane began to get used to her new duties. She was expected to do the Queen's bidding at all times, day or night, whether it was to converse, play cards or simply be in the same room working on her needlepoint. The Queen liked to have her maids of honour around her, especially Jane, whom she often singled out to read to her.

Whenever she could, Jane slipped away to see Delphine. Some days there was time to ride her in the spacious palace grounds and often Kit would accompany her, exercising one of the courtiers' mounts. Other days she only had time to quickly check on Delphine. But Kit was always there, and always willing to talk about the new theatre. Travelling players had visited Jane's home more than once, but in London, it seemed, the audience went to the players.

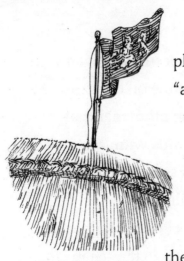

"If a play is to take place," Kit told her, "a flag flies from the top of the theatre. Then everyone hurries across the bridge or hires a boat to take them over the river. Of course, people who live on the south bank arrive on horseback." His face glowed. "It's a sight to see. And from tomorrow I'll be there every day."

"Oh," said Jane. She didn't know what to say. Kit had become a friend. She would miss him looking after Delphine, but she would miss his companionship, too.

"Delphine will be well cared for," Kit reassured her, as if reading her thoughts. "And maybe I'll see you at the theatre one day."

"I'd like that!" agreed Jane.

That afternoon, Jane and Katherine were sitting next to each other in the Queen's private chambers, working on their embroidery. Two of the other maids of honour were playing cards with the Queen. Another was playing a soft tune on the virginals. Sara was reading.

Jane moved her seat closer to Katherine. "Does the Queen ever go to the theatre?" she asked quietly.

But Sara overheard. "Of course not," she scoffed. "The players come to her."

Jane flushed. "I just thought..." She lowered her voice. "If she did," she whispered to Katherine, "would we go with her?"

"It will never happen," interrupted Sara again.

But she was wrong.

Barely a week later, Mrs Norris chivvied the girls at their midday meal. "Make haste," she urged. "You are all to be changed into your best dresses as soon as you have eaten."

"What's happening?" asked Jane.

Mrs Norris pursed her lips. "Her Majesty is going to the theatre."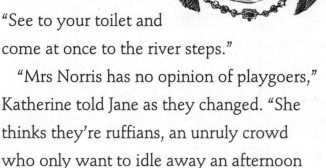

Jane caught her breath. "And we're to accompany her?"

Mrs Norris nodded. "See to your toilet and come at once to the river steps."

"Mrs Norris has no opinion of playgoers," Katherine told Jane as they changed. "She thinks they're ruffians, an unruly crowd who only want to idle away an afternoon drinking and shouting at the actors."

"But isn't that all part of the play?" said Jane.

Katherine laughed. "Mrs Norris doesn't think so!"

At the palace steps leading down to the river, the royal barge was waiting. Jane marvelled at the sight. The long, slender craft was beautifully painted in rich colours of crimson and gold. In the centre were two splendid cabins with glass windows. The Queen was already seated. Jane was handed in and found herself sitting on silk and satin cushions. She had never been in a boat before and wondered a little nervously what it would feel like:

the barge seemed very low in the water. But hardly had they left the palace steps than she began to enjoy the rhythmic pull of the twenty oarsmen who rowed them swiftly downriver. As they neared the landing stage, Jane saw lots more boats crossing the river, all full of eager playgoers.

Crowds thronged Bankside, but parted like magic to allow the Queen and her court to pass. Graciously, the Queen accepted their shouts of loyalty and praise.

The theatre
rose up in front of them. At the
top, a flag was flying. Jane felt a rush of
expectation. This was even more exciting
than watching the players at her own house.
She caught a glimpse of Kit helping an
elderly gentleman dismount from his horse.

She tried to catch
his eye but he didn't see her.

Inside, the theatre was filling up rapidly.
People were standing, sitting, calling to one
another. Some were buying refreshments
from hawkers selling beer and ale, nuts and
gingerbread.

The Queen was shown to her seat, close to the side of the stage. Her courtiers sat themselves down behind her. Mrs Norris kept a sharp eye on proceedings but even so, Sara managed to elbow Jane out of a seat with a clear view. Jane tried not to mind – it was wonderful just to be there, even if she was at the end of the row.

"Look above you!" said Katherine, beside her. Jane turned her attention

to the ceiling above the stage. Sun, moon and stars were painted in bright yellows and golds onto a vibrant blue background.

"It's called the heavens," whispered Katherine. "There's a trapdoor up there. Sometimes it opens and an actor is lowered on ropes!"

A trumpet sounded. The crowd hushed. The play was about to begin.

Although Jane could not see the actors on stage very well, she could see their comings and goings backstage through a door at the side. Each time the door opened, her attention was drawn to a young man beyond it, seated at a table. He was surrounded by sheets of paper and writing as though his life depended on it. He never seemed to notice the frantic activity taking place about him. Actors paced up and down muttering their lines to themselves. Last-minute costume details were hurriedly put right. Soon Jane found she was looking forward more to what was happening backstage than on the stage! At one point a small dog appeared.

46

Jane almost laughed out loud as the dog
neatly managed to avoid capture first by
one member of the cast, then by another.
Then, suddenly, it bounded
through the door and
headed straight towards
her. Jane jumped down
from her seat, stopped it
in its mad dash and scooped
it up in her arms. At once it
began licking her face joyfully.
Jane hugged it to her.

No one seemed to
have noticed. Sounds
of a fight issued
forth from the
stage, claiming
everyone's attention. But
the dog was starting to wriggle, desperate
to escape. Jane made for the door, and in
a moment she was backstage.

A cry of joy greeted her as Kit rushed forward. He didn't wait for explanations. He grabbed the dog.

"Thanks. It's needed in two minutes!" he said and disappeared.

Directly in front of Jane was the young man, still seated at his table. His pen scratched busily across the paper. Occasionally he paused, sat quite still for a moment, then continued.

Kit came back. "I've been helping out," he explained to Jane. "Will," he nodded towards the table, "is supposed to be calling the actors and dealing with dramas but he's too wrapped up in his writing! May I introduce you?" Jane nodded, speechless with excitement.

She was to meet a real, live playwright!

"Will," said Kit, "this is Lady Jane, maid of honour to the Queen. Lady Jane, this is my friend, Mr William Shakespeare."

A voice reached them clearly from the stage. "Hark! The thunder rolls. Great Jupiter is angry." Then there was a silence.

Kit groaned. "Will!" he cried. "They've forgotten to thunder. You'll have to go and tell them. I must return to my horses."

"Mmmm," agreed the writer. But his pen did not pause and he did not look up.

Again the voice came from the stage, urgent, louder. "THE THUNDER ROLLS…"

Kit looked stricken.

"I'll go," said Jane. "Where?"

"Up those steps," said Kit, "but…"

Jane ran for the stairs. "Keep going," called Kit, "until you reach the top."

Jane picked up her skirts and climbed swiftly. At the top there was a kind of hut. She wrenched open the door and burst into a small room. Two men were struggling to help a third into a purple robe, a silver crown and a mask. The third man appeared to be in pain, holding his stomach and groaning.

"Thunder!" gasped Jane.

At once, two of the men sprang across the room and set a huge cannonball rolling in a long wooden box. And then another. And another. The sound was deafening. The third man was now curled up on the floor. The thunder masked his cries but Jane saw that the poor fellow was moaning in agony.

In the centre of the room, the trapdoor

that Katherine had pointed out earlier was open. A giant carved eagle, held by ropes, was ready to descend.

The thunder ceased. "Hail to Jupiter!" a voice cried from the stage.

The two men looked at each other and then at their friend still writhing in pain on the floor. One picked up the robe. "Go to it," he said to the other.

"Not I," he replied, backing away.

"Jupiter!" cried the voice from below. Then the audience took up the cry. "Yes. Jupiter! Jupiter!"

Jane couldn't bear it. The whole play would be spoilt. She seized the robe, threw it on, loosed her hair, clamped the silver crown on her head and fixed the mask in place.

"Tell me what to do," she ordered.

The men stared at her. Then, while one sprang to the thunder once more, the other helped Jane take up her position.

The noise
ceased as
slowly,
gently, the
great eagle
with its
celestial rider
was lowered
into view.

The crowd
gasped. On stage,
the actors fell upon their
knees. "Hail, great Jupiter!"
they cried. "King of the gods! All hail!"

Only Katherine had noticed her absence,
Jane found to her relief when she returned
to her seat.

"Where did you go?" cried her friend. "You missed the best part. Jupiter descended from the sky!"

Jane smiled as she remembered the dizzying, exhilarating feeling of dangling high above the stage, swaying, flying.

"Heavens!" she said.

Fireships

Jane stood at the window looking out at the rain. Far below lay the port of Plymouth and its harbour, where her uncle had his merchant's offices. But Jane could not see them through the downpour. It's only a summer storm, she thought, but the rain seemed to contradict her, battering against the glass.

Jane turned back to the room. She trod softly across to the huge bed where her mother lay. As soon as word had reached

the Palace at Whitehall that Lady Anne
was gravely ill, the Queen had given Jane
permission to leave court. Such a long
journey it had been, because Lady Anne
was visiting her sister in Devon.

Since she had arrived, Jane had not
left her mother's bedside. She was very
frightened. She knew everyone feared for
Lady Anne's life. For days now the fever
had raged. Jane felt helpless in the face of
such sickness. She sat by the bed, took
her mother's hand into her own and leant
forward to rest her head on the coverlet.
Within seconds, she fell asleep.

When she awoke, sunlight filled the room. The door opened and her aunt entered.

"Come, my dear," she said. "Your uncle is about to leave for the harbour and wishes you to accompany him. The fresh air will do you good."

Jane hesitated. She was afraid to go, yet fearful to stay.

"I will remain with your mother," her aunt reassured her, "and you will not be long."

Down at the harbour, all was noise and activity. Ships crowded the quays. Goods were being loaded and unloaded. Her uncle pointed out one of his ships, the *Dolphin*. Jane recognized a young man who came dashing by: her eldest cousin, Ralph. He was chasing a chicken, which was squawking loudly in protest. Jane laughed at the sight but her uncle was displeased.

"Ralph!" he barked. "Be about your business."

At that moment Ralph flung himself forward, then stood up, the chicken held securely under one arm.

"Got you!" he said. Then he turned to his father and cousin. "I was just helping to load the *Dolphin*," he explained.

"Leave that to others," his father snapped. "It's not for you to be out here making a fool of yourself."

Ralph began to speak, then stopped. He handed the chicken to one of the boatmen and turned on his heel.

"Wait!" cried his father. "Since you're here, you can show your cousin around the harbour." He strode past his son into a nearby building.

Ralph bowed low. "Cousin Jane," he said, "it will be an honour." He paused until his father was out of earshot. "The old codger!"

Jane giggled. "That's not very respectful!"

"I know," agreed Ralph. "But I loathe sitting at a desk in the office. I long to be sailing."

He told Jane how his father's ships brought sugar and cotton from the West Indies and spices from the East.

"They call in here at Plymouth," he said, "and then continue up the English Channel. Sometimes I'm allowed to sail with them on the final part of their journey to London. But I can't even do that at the moment."

"Why not?" enquired Jane.

By now they had almost reached the end of the furthermost quay.

"That's why…" said Ralph, pointing.

Jane stared at the vast fleet of ships that filled the harbour mouth, each flying the English white and green flag.

"There's over a hundred of them," Ralph told Jane. "Waiting for the Armada."

Jane caught her breath. She had heard a lot about the Armada, the fleet of Spanish fighting ships. In recent months there had been talk of little else at court. King Philip of Spain was extremely angry with Queen Elizabeth for allowing her sailors (some said encouraging them) to attack Spanish galleons and steal their treasures. He was also furious that the Queen had dared to turn away from the Catholic faith. That was why the Armada was coming: to land Spanish soldiers on English soil and take over the country.

Jane shivered. "When are they expected?" she asked.

"No one knows," replied Ralph. "But we're ready." He pointed to one of the waiting ships. "That's the *Revenge*, the flagship, the one that will lead the others into battle. She's under the command of Sir Francis Drake. I'd give anything to sail with him."

"Is he famous?" asked Jane.

Ralph's eyes lit up. "He's sailed around the world," he told her. "At the moment he's on the hill above the harbour, playing bowls! Everyone thinks he's losing his mind, but from up there on the Hoe he can keep a look-out. He knows what he's doing."

When Jane returned to her aunt and uncle's house she found, to her joy, that her mother's fever had at last subsided. Lady Anne, though weak, was sitting up, supported by pillows. She was delighted to see Jane, but worried about her having left the court.

"The Queen insisted that I came," Jane reassured her. "And it is so good to see you so much better!"

Each day that followed, Lady
Anne made such good progress that soon
she was able to leave her bed and sit by
the window to watch Jane riding by on her
cousins' fat old pony.

One hot afternoon Jane waved to her
mother and rode on up and up to the top
of the hill behind the house. She was
beginning to feel restless. Her aunt was kind

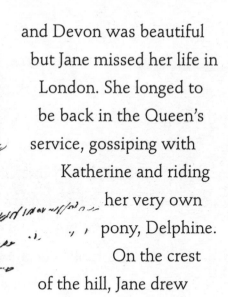

and Devon was beautiful
but Jane missed her life in
London. She longed to
be back in the Queen's
service, gossiping with
Katherine and riding
her very own
pony, Delphine.
On the crest
of the hill, Jane drew
the pony to a halt and gazed out
over the bay. A ship was just coming into
sight around the headland, then another,
and another: a flotilla of ships. Jane sat up,
startled. There were pennants and ensigns
in abundance, all different colours, but from
every mast also flew a red flag with a gold
cross. The Spanish flag.

The Armada was coming!

She turned her pony and sped back down
to the house.

*　　*　　*

That night at the evening meal, the talk was all of the invading fleet making its way up the English Channel.

"They say Drake saw the Armada coming," said Ralph, "but calmly finished his game of bowls and then turned his attention to beating the Spaniards."

"The man's a fool!" declared Jane's uncle. "Even now he's doing nothing. What is he waiting for?"

"The wind and the tide," murmured Ralph, so low that only Jane, sitting next to him, could hear. Aloud, Ralph said, "Sir Francis plans to sail at nightfall, coming in behind the Spanish ships and taking them by surprise."

His father grunted his disapproval. "Well, at least we can get the *Dolphin* on her way up the Channel to the merchants awaiting her goods in London," he said.

Shocked faces greeted this news. "But it's far too dangerous," Jane's aunt protested. "Surely we must wait."

"I've bided my time long enough!" cried her husband. "Ralph, you can take command. You're always telling me how capable you are."

Ralph's face shone with excitement.

"Can I go with him?" said Jane quickly.

There was a silence. Then came from Jane's mother and aunt an outpouring of reasons why the idea was not to be considered; was entirely impossible. A mere girl on a boat in the English Channel teeming with fighting ships?

But her uncle guffawed. "You've got spirit!" he cried. "I'll say that for you, my lady."

Taking heart from this response, Jane reminded her family that she needed to get back to London with all speed; that in her position as maid of honour she should be at the Queen's side at such a time as this. "Now that you're well, of course," she added, turning to her mother.

Lady Anne spread her hands helplessly.

Ralph was on Jane's side too. "Remember," he assured his aunt, "the *Dolphin* is a merchant ship. We have nothing to fear."

And so it was decided. Jane was to sail!

For the first few days, as Ralph had predicted, the *Dolphin* sailed unchallenged along the Channel.

Jane stood on deck, holding on tightly, getting used to the pitch and roll. It was very different from the smooth passage of the royal barge on the River Thames.

Below, in the Captain's cabin, she made herself useful, tidying charts and papers, making sure writing materials were secured so that they didn't slide off the table as the ship dipped and rose in the waves.

Now and then she heard gunfire, but it was always in the distance and the crew took little notice. On the third day it seemed much closer, and then came an enormous explosion.

"It's the *San Salvador*!" cried a seaman as Jane struggled in the fierce wind to get up on deck to see what was happening. "It's blown up!"

Cheering broke out all across the ship. Jane could see the Spanish boat clearly, its masts broken, its prow split, flames licking its sides and men jumping, screaming, into the sea. She turned away, sickened.

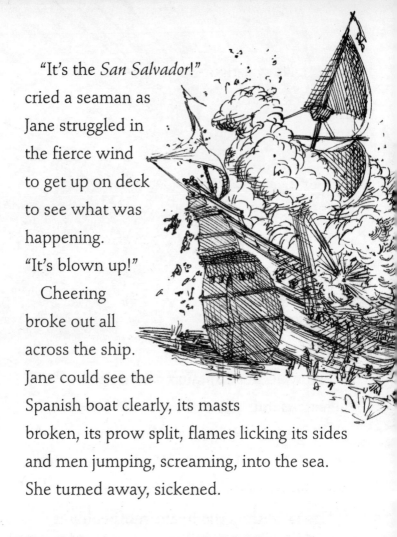

The following morning, Ralph gave orders for Jane to stay below deck. Gunfire raged throughout the day. Twice, Jane was sent reeling across the cabin. At noon, Ralph came down. He was tight-lipped and unshaven.

"What's happening?" cried Jane.

"The Armada is sailing in a crescent formation," Ralph explained. "Our ships are lower in the water and faster but we dare to attack only the outer edges. If we try to storm the centre, we will be surrounded."

He spoke as if he was taking part, thought Jane. "But Sir Francis Drake will outwit them?" she said.

Ralph made no reply.

"And we're just a merchant ship," persisted Jane. "We're not in the battle."

"We might as well be," said Ralph bitterly. "We've been ordered to drop anchor. We're not allowed to continue our journey."

There was such despair in his voice that fear flipped through Jane's body. The *Dolphin* was no match against a Spanish galleon. If one came close, there would be no escape.

71

All afternoon she waited for news. She tried to keep herself busy, writing up the day's events in her journal. But why had they been told to stop? What use could a merchant ship be in a battle?

Towards evening, Ralph came below deck once again. Taking no notice of Jane, he began to collect papers. He paced around the cabin, glancing briefly at each document before thrusting it into a large leather bag.

Jane watched in silence. Her cousin was so intent upon his task, she did not wish to disturb him. But what was he doing? Surely this was not the moment to be sorting papers?

Unable to hold herself back any longer, she said, "Can I help?"

Ralph picked up the *Dolphin*'s logbook. "There isn't much time," he told her. "The Armada is now at anchor in the port of Calais. On land, near by, the Duke of Parma is waiting with an army of Spanish soldiers. If they succeed in boarding the Armada, they'll cross the Channel and England will be lost."

He pushed the logbook into the bag and fastened the clasp. "But," he continued, "Sir Francis Drake has a plan."

Jane wondered at the stricken look on his face.

"That's good, isn't it?" she ventured.

"Eight ships are to be set on fire," said Ralph, "and sent into the midst of the Armada to burn it down." He paused. "One of them is the *Dolphin*."

Jane's head reeled. "But why...?"

There was no time for further
explanations. Quickly, Jane was transferred
to the *Revenge*, from where she helped
the crew to pass bundles of wood, bits of
rope, anything that would burn, into
the *Dolphin*. She could only imagine
what this must mean to Ralph: to
lose his father's ship on his first
command. At midnight, the
wind changed, blowing
towards the Armada.

The eight ships
were let loose.

Aboard the *Revenge*
the two crews stood,
silent. Jane strained her
eyes to see. Suddenly,
the first fireship flared
into action. Then
another, and another.
Flames lit up the sky.

The devil-burners
closed in among
the towering galleons.
"They've cut their
anchor cables!" shouted
Ralph. "We have the Armada
on the run!"

Spanish ships scuttled in all directions, blundering into each other, desperate to escape the fireships. But the wind picked up strength, fanning the flames. Sea and sky were ablaze.

Jane watched until her eyes would stay open no longer. Then, huddled into a corner of the deck, she slept.

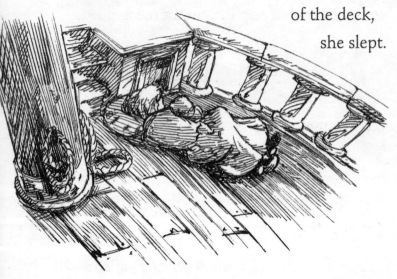

Ralph found her at sunrise. "The Armada's crescent is broken!" he cried triumphantly. "Its ships have been driven out into the North Sea."

Excitedly, he told her of the *Revenge*'s plan: to hound the Spanish ships northwards to ensure they did not return.

"And I am to go with them," he declared.

Jane smiled at his obvious joy.

She was to be rowed ashore, where a groom and horse were waiting. Her job would be to carry an important message to London.

"Tell the Queen," Sir Francis Drake instructed her, "God blew and the Armada was scattered. Tell her, England is safe!"

Long Live the Queen!

Hot, dusty and tired, Jane arrived at St James's Palace in London. Weary though she was, she requested to see the Queen at once.

"Her Majesty cannot be disturbed," said Mrs Norris, fussing over bed linen in the laundry.

"But I have a message for her," pleaded Jane.

"It will have to wait," Mrs Norris told her, folding another sheet. "Her Majesty is in consultation with her ministers. You may not be aware, but this country is in constant threat of invasion."

"Not any more!" cried Jane.

Mrs Norris tutted. "As if you would know," she said, bustling Jane out of the laundry. "You must, of course, change into fresh clothes," she added – not unkindly – as she swept away. "And then resume your duties."

Jane could not think of delay. As soon as Mrs Norris had disappeared from view, she made her way quickly to the Queen's private chambers.

Two footmen stood outside.

"The Queen has sent for me," declared Jane boldly. "Please open the door."

To her relief, one of the footmen leapt to obey.

As she entered the room, the conversation came to an abrupt halt. For a second, Jane faltered as all eyes turned upon her. She drew a deep breath, curtsied and spoke.

"Your Majesty, please forgive this 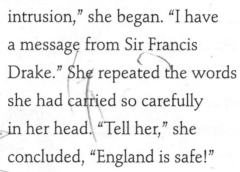 intrusion," she began. "I have a message from Sir Francis Drake." She repeated the words she had carried so carefully in her head. "Tell her," she concluded, "England is safe!"

 Jane was not prepared for the silence that followed. She hadn't thought what to expect. Cheering, perhaps? Eager questions? But not this – nothing.

The Queen was the first to speak. Her tone was cool. "How came you by this information?" she enquired.

"I was there!" said Jane. "I saw the Armada scattered."

One of the ministers laughed outright. "A maid like you?" he jeered.

Others joined in, mocking. "A fanciful tale! Do you not think we would have heard of such a victory by now?"

Jane was furious. "My lords," she cried, "I have ridden with all speed to acqaint you with this news. No one could have journeyed more quickly."

Tears sprang to her eyes. Her whole body ached. She longed for sleep. But not before she had delivered her message. She would make them listen. She turned to the Queen and poured out the story of her departure from Plymouth, the skirmishes in the Channel, the sending-out of the fireships and the scattering of the Armada.

As she finished, the Queen rose. "Thank you," she said. "Go and rest now."

Jane knew she was being dismissed but she could not help herself. "Your Majesty does believe me?" she asked.

The Queen smiled. "You have indeed brought us splendid news."

Then why, thought Jane, as she retired to her bedchamber, did the Queen's response give her a feeling of unease?

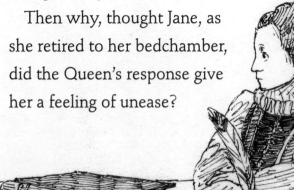

When Jane woke, Katherine was at her side. "You've been asleep a whole night and a day," she told her friend. "You didn't even wake when we came in."

Jane sat up. Her head felt thick and heavy.

"Tell me everything," ordered Katherine. "I've missed you enormously and I'm very glad you're back. But what have you been doing? Have you really sailed on the *Revenge* and helped Sir Francis Drake?"

Jane did her best to explain the story all over again. "So now England is completely out of danger," she finished.

Katherine looked doubtful. "That's not what I've heard here at court," she said. "The Duke of Parma is still hoping to cross the Channel with sixteen thousand men. They say London could be attacked from the east, at Tilbury."

Jane was horrified. "But Sir Francis said we were safe!"

Katherine laughed. "You and your friend Sir Francis," she teased. "Anyway, I was instructed to tell you the Queen wants to see you the minute you wake—"

"Why didn't you say?" exclaimed Jane, struggling into her clothes.

The Queen received Jane alone. "Official reports have now reached us regarding the flight of the Armada, just as you described," she said. "Even so, tomorrow I go to Tilbury. I have determined to visit my troops who are standing by in the event of invasion. You are all to accompany me."

So the rumours were true, thought Jane, her heart sinking. England was not out of danger yet.

At the evening meal, the talk was all of the Queen's visit to Tilbury.

"Everyone is to go," said Katherine. "There is to be a procession and music."

"It's madness," declared Sara. "The Queen should stay here where it's safe."

"She wishes to support her troops," defended Jane.

"Troops?" laughed Sara. "A few hundred trained soldiers – and the rest, farmers, ploughmen and suchlike from the country."

"She wants to be among her people, whoever they are," Jane insisted.

"Plenty of her people support the King of Spain and wish her dead," retorted Sara. "Anything could happen."

*   *   *

The following morning,
the Queen and her court boarded
the royal barge, which was to take them
down the Thames to the docks at Tilbury.
Then the Queen would ride to the nearby
camp to inspect the foot soldiers and cavalry
assembled there.

Jane was dressed entirely in white. The
Queen also wore a riding habit of white
satin, and when they arrived at the docks,
a high-stepping white horse was brought
forward.

"Tempest!" cried Jane.

The Queen smiled. "I would have none other," she declared. She put on a silver breastplate and mounted. Jane was to lead the procession, and one of the guards handed her a white cushion to hold. Upon it rested a silver helmet. When all was ready, the procession moved off, with Jane walking just ahead of Tempest. Crowds lined the route. Drummers beat the rhythm of a rousing march. Pipers played. Banners and streamers flew.

Jane's hands trembled
from excitement as
she tried to keep up
a steady pace.

There were
shouts of "Lord,
preserve our Queen!"
intermingled with cheers
and clapping as they passed. Children were
hoisted onto shoulders. Onlookers gazed
out of high windows. Dogs barked.

As they rounded the first
corner, Jane glanced behind
her. Tempest was
stepping out
proudly. Her
Majesty rode him
like a warrior queen
going into battle,
she thought.

She turned her attention back to
the front and a flicker of movement
up to her left caught her eye. In an
open window, high above the procession,
a man was lifting something to his shoulder.

A musket!

Seconds before the shot rang out,
Jane turned and threw the
silver helmet and
its cushion at
Tempest. He
reared, as she
knew he would,
putting his body
between the bullet and
the Queen. The cushion
took the force of the
gunfire, exploding
into the air.

A thousand feathers spun.

The crowd scattered in panic. Some fell back, others surged forward, knocking Jane to the ground. Guards quickly surrounded the Queen and forced the crowd away from her. Jane's fingers closed around the silver helmet where it had fallen. She stood up, her legs far from steady. The guards' horses were plunging all about her but she could see that the Queen was safe in her saddle. Jane reached up to pat Tempest's neck, reassuring him until the snorting of his nostrils grew quieter.

The Queen, against all advice, insisted on proceeding. She leant forward. "Thank you," she said and Jane knew she meant more than the calming of her horse. "Are you able to continue?"

Jane nodded.

The way ahead was cleared. Jane took her place. The procession moved on.

* * *

Three months later, Jane sat beside Katherine in St Paul's Cathedral, reliving that day at Tilbury.

"Let tyrants fear," the Queen had told her troops. "I know I have the body of a weak and feeble woman, but I have the heart and stomach of a king, and think it foul scorn that Parma or Spain, or any prince of Europe, should dare to invade the borders of my realm."

And no one *had* dared to invade England. The Duke of Parma had not crossed the Channel, and the English army had been disbanded and sent home to bring in the harvest. Now, here they were in St Paul's, statesmen, courtiers, Queen and people, all giving thanks for such a great victory.

Jane shifted in her seat. The cathedral was packed. Crowds of people lined the streets outside, too. Among them, Jane had spied Kit helping calm one of the royal greys. She'd smiled to herself. Always there to lend a hand with a horse!

Inside were her whole family, her mother and father, brothers and sisters, her aunt and uncle and cousins. Ralph had acted with such courage in the defeat of the Armada that he had been invited to make his career in the Navy; and his father had been given a brand-new merchant ship to make up for the loss of the *Dolphin*.

At a given signal, Jane stood up, clutching a piece of paper in her hand. Then, loudly and clearly, though the backs of her knees were wobbling in a terrifying manner, she read out her poem "The Scattering of the Armada", which she had written especially for the occasion.

The Queen smiled as Jane sat down.

The service was almost over. Her Majesty rose and read her own prayer of thanksgiving, finishing with a plea for all her subjects to be grateful for their glorious deliverance.

A great shout filled the cathedral.

"Long live the Queen!" roared the people. "Vivat Regina!"

Long may I serve her, thought Jane, and raised her voice to join the throng.

"Vivat! Vivat Regina!"

June Crebbin is the author of a number of books for children, including *Invasion* – a story about the Norman Conquest – four Merryfield Hall Riding School stories and several picture books for younger children.

June very much enjoyed writing *The Queen's Maid*, which is set in a particularly exciting period of history. As part of her research she visited Kenilworth Castle, Plymouth Hoe and of course the Globe Theatre in London, a replica of the original. Open to the sky, it enables you to experience a Shakespearian play very much as the Elizabethans did – but without the smell of horses! June has two grown-up sons and two grandsons and lives in Leicestershire.

James de la Rue has illustrated several books over the past few years, but none of them have featured quite so many ostentatious neck ruffs as this one. He can only imagine how annoying it would have been, all those centuries ago, to be late for the first production of a new Shakespeare play only to realize that one's theatre ruff was in the laundry! James lives in Nottinghamshire with his wife and daughter.